THE TRASH CAN REVIEW

THE TRASH CAN REVIEW

Joanne E. De Jonge

Illustrated by Timothy Foley

William B. Eerdmans Publishing Company
Grand Rapids, Michigan

Copyright © 1992 by Wm. B. Eerdmans Publishing Co.
255 Jefferson Ave. S.E., Grand Rapids, Mich. 49503

Printed in the United States of America

ISBN 0-8028-5071-5

This book is dedicated to the Lord of all
Who made the earth and everything in it
and charged us with its keeping.

Contents

A HEAP OF RUBBISH

Trash Can Tally Reveals Garbage Glut

The word is out; we can't keep a lid on our trash. We have a garbage glut.

The average American — kid as well as adult — now tosses between three and four pounds of trash every day. While a few pounds may not seem like much, they tally up to a disgustingly impressive total in a hurry.

Save your trash for one month and you'll find that it weighs about as much as you do. But it takes up more space because it isn't as compact as you are. Save it for a year and you'll have over half a ton of the yucky stuff. Imagine your bedroom with a year's trash in it!

If you kept all your trash from the day you entered kindergarten to the day you left sixth grade, you'd be able to pack a classroom to overflowing. Collect for a lifetime and you could fill the typical school gym.

So what's one dinky school gymful in an entire lifetime? No problem if you're the only kid on earth. But add your friends' trash to your own and you could probably fill up a gym in short order. Or multiply one gymful by the number of kids in the world and you have a serious problem.

But we've been generating garbage for years and never ran into trouble. Why do we have a problem now?

First and most obvious, we're running out of places to put trash and things to do with it. And we're discovering that out of sight doesn't always mean out of our lives. Last year's sneakers can come back in many forms to haunt us. (See Section Two.)

But more basic and less obvious to many people, we're trashing a Creation that isn't ours to trash. And we're hypocritical about it to boot. Every day we thank God for his gifts, and then throw more than three pounds of them away. (See Section Three.)

So what's the answer? Nothing simple, that's for sure; but there are things that we can do.

First, we should be aware of the problem. ~~That's what the first two sections of *Trash Can Review* are about.~~ These ~~pages~~ facts may be depressing, but they're not the end of the story.

Christians should give special thought to their reactions and responsibilities. ~~That's what "A Word from Our Sponsor" is all about.~~ *so that's part of what I'll be talking to you about.*

Then, each of us can do a little something. ~~That's what the rest of *Trash Can Review* concentrates on. Read on for the whole review.~~ *And that's where you guys come in.*

Typical Trash Tells Tales

Although trash cans don't talk and no one has heard a garbage pail gossip, the stuff thrown into those containers says a lot about the person(s) who threw it. Consider this trash from a family of three.

You See	You Know
Empty cat food cans	They have a cat
Kitty litter in a newspaper	The cat stays inside
Food scraps	No garbage disposal
Potato peels, apple cores, bones	They eat fresh foods
Cigarette butts	Someone smokes
Comic books	Kid in the house
School papers	Kid gets A's & B's
Empty acne cream tube	Kid has zits
News magazines, daily papers	They keep up with news
Barely worn tennies	Kid's feet are growing
More barely worn clothes	Whole kid is growing
Several AA batteries	Someone fixed a Walkman
Three church bulletins	They each read separate bulletins
Potato chip bags, candy bar wrappers	Someone snacks a lot
Lots of bags	They shop a lot
Box and packing	They bought a new TV

Doesn't that make you wonder what *your* trash says about *you?*

Fun (or Not-So-Much-Fun) Fact

There's even junk orbiting the earth, tossed out or lost during space missions. It ranges from plastic bags of human waste to one lost camera. Some experts say that there's over a million pounds out there.

A Weighty Problem

IT'S YOUR TURN

Find out how you weigh in against the "average" trash tosser. Make a garbage bag your constant companion for the next twenty-four hours. Every time you toss something, toss it into that bag.

Don't forget your "hidden" trash: eggshells from your breakfast, ~~the milk carton from your school lunch,~~ your share of potato peelings and cans used in making supper, ~~part of the newspaper if you read it, and even a piece of the dog food can.~~

After one full day, weigh the bag carefully; then fill in the blanks below.

DATE: _____

MY PERSONAL TRASH

WEIGHED ___ POUNDS.

Junkyard Jargon

Trash, garbage, junk, rubbish, refuse, etc., etc.; what's the difference? Technically speaking, there may be some. For our purposes, all those words mean the same thing: stuff you throw away.

Your Very Own Trash Can Tale

Want to find out a lot about yourself? Mess around in your trash.

It's best to use your whole family's weekly trash. But if you're really squeamish, use the bagful you just collected. (See "A Weighty Problem," this section.)

Lay down a few newspapers so that the garbage "juice" doesn't seep all over the place. Then dump the trash out, sort through it, and see what tales it tells. Here are a few questions to get you started.

What did you eat? Many fast foods? Do you have a garbage disposal?

Where have you shopped? What have you bought?

How are your grades? What homework was tossed?

Do you get lots of junk mail? Do you open it?

Did you go to any movies? Read any magazines or newspapers? Write any love letters?

Is anyone outgrowing clothes? Wearing them out? Just tossing them?

What shampoo or soap do you use? Does someone shave with disposable razors? Color her hair? Treat zits?

Your Trash Can Tally Sheet

Write Your Own Trash Can Tale

Your Trash Can Tally Sheet

Write Your Own Trash Can Tale

It's All Garbage

IT'S YOUR TURN

At least twenty pieces of typical trash are hidden in this can. Draw a circle around the items when you find them. Sometimes they read forward; at other times backward, up, down, or diagonally. Can you find them?

```
T O S N T S P O X B R H G V V M
L V O Z R V B D L C A N V T B A
Q Q I S R N Q M D T Z G T Y A Q
U H O M B A K A E B O T T L E K
L A L H B X L C D O R Y M E F J
A S M H T F J M E X S Z U T Z L
U N L E X Y U L Y M R S I T H L
C G M D K W Y M I E S C X E Q V
R A P A P E R M K I E U Y R B T
G I I Q I Q B A T T E R Y Z S K
Y F D U N L E G P U Z Z L E I B
G J C Q H N Z A C P Q D T Q G V
U J L P S V F Z O K E L Q M K B
J E A E I Y Q I R L I R E R E B
Q Q F Z Y R A N E W S P A P E R
M M T X W Y E E T P L M V J N Q
Y H U W Q L P P H N P A Z J G B
```

(Answer key on page 62)

Where in the World Is "Away"?

A mini-mountain of trash sits at your feet or in your trash can not too many feet away from you. What do you do with all that rubbish? Conventional wisdom says that you throw it away. Put it in front of the house on the proper day and it disappears; the trash hauler takes it away.

What is "away"?

Is "away" a wonderful place where sneakers are vaporized, candy bar wrappers are crushed to nothingness, and the remains of yesterday's lunch disappear without a trace? Maybe "away" is a gaping hole in the earth that eats trash like most of us eat pizza; can't get enough of it. Better yet, perhaps "away" is a magical door that opens onto space. We fling our trash through the "away" door, and it is sucked into the far reaches of the universe, never to be seen again.

Where in the world is "away"?

One thing we know for sure about "away"; it is *not* here. Nothing can be here and away at the same time; if it's here, it's not away. So "away" is not here. But if you leave here and go away, when you get there you'll say that "there" is "here" and "away" is never here, so "away" isn't "there" either.

Confusing, isn't it? It all boils down to this: You may search through all Creation, but you will never find "away." THERE IS NO "AWAY." When you throw something away, it does not magically disappear.

That mini-mountain of trash must go somewhere; "away" is not an option. We know, you'll still throw it away. But exactly where will it go? What will happen to it? "Gagging on Garbage" (Section Two) may give you some clues.

Throughout this week we'll be looking at the issue of garbage, trash and other stuff. Just some things to think about

GAGGING ON GARBAGE

Forgotten, but Not Gone

Remember the sneakers you threw "away" last year because they were too small? You probably never gave them another thought. But now that you've read "Where in the World Is 'Away'?" you may be wondering exactly where they are if they're not "away." Those sneakers, like all the trash you've thrown away in the past several years, may be forgotten, but they're probably not gone. Chances are that one of three things happened to them: they were dumped into a landfill, they were incinerated, or they were tossed into the sea.

Chances are greatest that they were dumped into a landfill. Approximately 80 percent of our household trash finds its final resting place in a landfill.

If your sneakers are at this very moment sitting in a landfill, you might still be able to recognize them as your sneakers. True, they'd be pretty gross, having been buried under tons of junk, but they probably haven't changed that much yet. They certainly haven't fallen apart completely.

People who study garbage say that junk dumped into a landfill simply doesn't fall apart as quickly as we would like to think. They've found newspapers more than ten years old and yet perfectly readable. Carrots dumped next to the papers could have been scrubbed clean and eaten, if anyone had the stomach for them. If carrots can

take years to fall apart in a dump, certainly your sneakers are in pretty good shape yet.

Of course, they may be leaking a little sneaker juice by this time. Rainwater has trickled into the earth, soaked your sneakers, and oozed farther downward. Now that water is carrying some of the shoe color, chemicals used to make that color, and any other rotten "goodies" that may have infested those sneakers. If that landfill leaks, pity the poor worm making its home below; it had sneaker juice among other garbage goodies for breakfast. (For more on dumps and landfills, see "An Open and Shut Case" and "A Problem That Can't Be Buried," this section.)

If you live near an incinerator, your shoes may be but a dim memory. They may have been trucked directly to that giant furnace, tossed in with tons of other junk, and burned beyond recognition. Perhaps someone downwind had a whiff of burned sneakers sometime last year, your tennies' final farewell. Of course, the sneakers probably left some ash, but you couldn't hope to recognize that as a former pair of shoes. (For more on incinerators see "A Burning Issue," this section.)

Perhaps your sneakers are resting comfortably in a watery grave at the bottom of the sea. If you live within striking distance of an ocean, your trash just may be hauled out there and dumped. We can't say for sure what condition they are in, but I would guess that they're still recognizable. Or maybe the tops have fallen apart, but the soles are still there. Or maybe, just maybe, they're home for some hermit crab.

We don't know much about what happens to trash dumped at sea. What we do know is not pretty. (See "Sixpacks at Sea," this section.) In fact, we don't even know much about those sea-going creatures on whom we dump the junk. Certainly, a hermit crab wasn't created for life in a soaked sneaker.

Hermit crabs, sneaker ash, and sneaker juice aside, the point is this: although you threw those shoes away last year, chances are that they still aren't completely gone. They may even be wearable yet. Doesn't that make you wonder about the rest of your trash?

IT'S YOUR TURN

Sixpacks at Sea

We don't know much about what happens to the millions (some say billions) of pounds of trash we dump into our oceans every year. But we do know that some of it is killing God's little creatures. Turtles gobble up plastic bags, thinking that they're jellyfish.

The bags then clog up their digestive systems and the turtles die.

Plastic six-pack rings are especially dangerous. Marine birds and mammals as well as fish become stuck in the rings. The creatures grow; the rings don't. Eventually the creatures are strangled by their plastic "necklaces."

It has been estimated that a million sea birds, 100,000 marine mammals, and 50,000 fur seals are killed every year from eating plastic or being strangled by it.

Before you toss a plastic six-pack ring, do God's little creatures a favor. Take a scissors and snip the thing apart. Then nothing can strangle in it.

A Problem That Can't Be Buried

For years we've buried trash without a thought. Suddenly we're gagging on garbage and don't know where to go with it. Are our dumps really full? What's the problem?

First, we're realizing that our old dumps weren't very sightly or safe. Trash blew all over the place. Dumps didn't smell very good. They leaked toxic juices into nearby soil and groundwater. (See "A Battery of Chemicals" and "An Open and Shut Case," this section). We're trying to clean up our act, but this can be very expensive.

Second, a filled landfill can't be used for just anything. A park might be fine, but the land generally can't be farmed. Often, the site is too unstable for buildings. Should we use God's good earth simply to bury trash?

Third, more and more people are absolutely insisting that no landfill be placed near them. (See "NIMBYs Edge Out TWABALs in Great Trash Race," this section.) They don't want dump trucks rolling past their houses all day, or yucky messes, or the threat of sneaker-juice water and smelly air. People want to throw their trash away — far, far away.

Yes, there's a problem. Landfills are closing and we can't find places for new ones.

Is there a solution? Read Sections Four, Five, and Six. That may give you ideas on just what to do with your next pair of tennies.

An Open and Shut Case

What's the difference between a dump and a sanitary landfill?

A dump usually refers to an old-fashioned hole in the ground where people throw trash. It looks like a dump since nothing is done to cover the junk thrown on  top of the heap. The bottom of the heap often leaks "garbage juice" — rainwater that has collected toxic chemicals and yucky stuff from the trash — into the soil below or water nearby.

A sanitary landfill is the newer version of the old dump. Dirt is bulldozed on top of each daily contribution of trash so that the sights and smells are not as revolting. The bottom of a landfill has a waterproof lining to hold the garbage juice. Modern gadgets monitor nearby soil and water for pollution, and pipes siphon  away any gas that may collect.

Need we ask which is healthier? It's an open and shut case.

A Burning Issue

What to do when you run out of landfill space? Simple; burn your trash! Several cities have built incinerators as their answer to the garbage glut.

Simply put, an incinerator is a huge furnace in which the city's trash is burned. True, the ash that's left must be buried, but there's a lot less ash than there was trash. And many cities use the heat from the incinerator as a power source. Sounds great, doesn't it?

But there are some problems. The ash that's left is often highly toxic; where can that be buried? Fumes from the burning trash also contain poisons; scrubbers must be built into the incinerator's smokestacks to catch those fumes. This whole business can be very expensive, and we still don't know how safe it is.

Even if all our questions about incinerators were answered and they were a great solution to the garbage glut, one issue would still remain: Is it right to throw so much away? That's the real issue.

Garbage Juice for Breakfast

Fresh Kills on Staten Island, New York, is one of the largest city dumps in the world. According to New York officials, this dump leaks more than a million gallons of contaminated garbage juice into nearby groundwater *every day*.

IT'S YOUR TURN

Track Your Trash

Want to really personalize your garbage and find out exactly where those sneakers go? Then talk to your trash hauler.

Find out what day your trash is taken away and lie in wait for the hauler. As soon as you hear that big truck rumble up to your house, run outside and ask the person who's emptying your trash can exactly where the stuff goes.

Does it go to a dump or a landfill? Which one? Where is it?

Is it incinerated? What happens to the ash?

Is it hauled out to sea and then thrown overboard? How far out is it hauled?

Don't be shy about asking. Trash haulers have been questioned before; they should gladly give you the information.

If your family takes its own trash away, go along sometime and take a good look around. You'll be looking at your sneakers' second home.

Next time you throw something "away," you can picture exactly where it goes and what happens (or doesn't happen) to it.

A Battery of Chemicals

That flashlight battery you tossed into the trash yesterday may be harmful to someone's health. Experts say that batteries contain very toxic chemicals that ooze into landfills or waft out on incinerator exhaust. (We can only guess what happens to sea-tossed batteries.) The list of battery ingredients sounds like the top ten of toxic trash: cadmium, lead, lithium, manganese dioxide, mercury, nickel, silver, and zinc. How would you like that in your soup? It's in our garbage juice.

No one battery has all these little delights, but each combines a few choice ingredients. We're talking about batteries that power cameras, watches, flashlights, calculators, Walkmen, remote control devices, and some of your favorite toys and games. Americans trash about 2.5 billion of these little chemical composites every year.

Thirty Seconds to Live

A dump in Florida leaked so much toxic juice into groundwater that it "killed" a nearby lake. Although the dump is now closed, a healthy fish thrown into that lake dies within thirty seconds.

IT'S YOUR TURN

Down in the Dumps

See for yourself how long it takes trash to fall apart in a dump.

Find a space outside where you can dig two holes. They don't have to be very big. Make them about six inches deep.

Lay a small brown paper bag flat in one of the holes and cover it with dirt. Lay a plastic bag in the other hole and cover that with dirt, too. Mark the place you have dug so that you can find them easily.

After one week, dig up both bags. Is either starting to degrade?

_____

Bury them again and dig them up again after one month. Can you see any difference?

_____

Which bag, if any, is starting to fall apart?

_____

Continue to check the bags periodically and rebury them, until one bag starts to fall apart.

How long does it take for one of the bags to begin to degrade?

_____

Which bag degrades first?

_____

Which bag looks like it won't degrade at all?

_____

Foam, Sweet Foam

The jury is still out
on the vices and virtues of polystyrene foam,
often called Styrofoam.

There's much to be said in its favor. It's lightweight and convenient, and it insulates well. Some stores and companies will recycle foam trays and containers. And many experts say that it's less polluting to manufacture than the paper products that would take its place.

Yet foam takes a lot of space for its weight and won't fall apart in a landfill. It's made from petrochemicals, a nonrenewable resource. And if it doesn't use CFCs (ozone destroying chemicals) in its manufacture, it often uses pentane or butane, low-level pollutants.

Foam, sweet foam; is it a bane or a blessing? Individuals must decide.

IT'S YOUR TURN

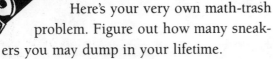

Multiply Your Mess

Here's your very own math-trash problem. Figure out how many sneakers you may dump in your lifetime.

Fill in the first blank with the number of sneakers (that's sneakers, not pairs) you have in your closet (and your gym locker at school) right now. Figure that as the total number of sneakers you'll use this year.

You're probably at your peak sneaker power right now. You didn't wear them as a baby; chances are that you'll wear fewer as a senior citizen. That's why you multiply the first number by one-half. That will give you an idea of the average number of sneakers you'll use per year in your lifetime. (Obviously, this is *not* an accurate or scientific tabulation.)

Take the first answer you got (the average number of sneakers per year), and put that in the first space on the second line. Figure that your lifetime will be the biblical threescore and ten years. Multiply your first answer by 70. That will give you the number of sneakers you may dump in your lifetime.

$$\underline{\hspace{3cm}} \times \tfrac{1}{2} = \underline{\hspace{3cm}}.$$
$$\underline{\hspace{3cm}} \times 70 = \underline{\hspace{3cm}}.$$

Now think for a minute about where all those sneakers go. Read "Forgotten, but Not Gone" (this section) if you haven't already done so.

Where Have All the Sneakers Gone?

Eighty percent of household trash is put into a _____.

Some cities _____ their trash, leaving fumes and ash.

Millions of pounds of trash are thrown into the _____ each year.

NIMBYs Edge Out TWABALs in Great Trash Race

No one knew that the great race had begun; yet everyone was in it, and almost everyone was a TWABAL.

The great race is the race to trash Planet Earth; everyone is in it because everyone throws away trash. At first almost everyone figured, "There Will Always Be A Landfill" (TWABAL); no problem, lots of space, dump the junk and it will disappear.

Gradually, some people began to recognize problems; dumps were dirty and smelly, and could be hazardous to their health. And so the NIMBY movement was born.

When a public hearing on a new landfill was scheduled, a NIMBY or two picketed with signs: Not In My Back Yard (NIMBY). In other words, "I don't want that mess near me; put it somewhere else."

Some trashers became TWABAL-NIMBYs. They believed that there was plenty of room for a new landfill, so much room that it didn't have to be near them. Trash someone else's back yard.

Then the NIMBY movement exploded. Understandably, no one wanted a landfill nearby; everyone wanted it someplace else. Almost everyone became a NIMBY.

That's when the NIMBYs began to edge out the TWABALs in the great race. If people do not want a dump in their back yard, where will a new landfill be placed? Perhaps there won't always be a landfill. Trashers quietly dropped their TWABAL labels as they thought out their NIMBY positions.

Somewhere along the line, the Great Trash Race took a disquieting turn. As the NIMBY movement gathered strength, whole countries took on that label. Wealthy countries like the United States began to pay other countries to take their garbage. They exported tons of trash, including hazardous wastes, to poor countries that couldn't afford to say "No."

That's about where the Great Trash Race stands today. NIMBYs have edged out TWABALs. Whole countries have become NIMBYs and are dumping on poor countries.

This report of a race that has no winners could be very discouraging; but trash watchers report two recent developments. These could affect the whole course of the race.

First, kids have become active participants. They've proved to be more effective than their parents in slowing down the race by reducing the amount of trash they throw out and convincing adults to do the same. Kids have learned to use things that the older generation used to dump. And kids have persuaded schools, corporations, and communities to set up recycling programs.

Second, the Christian community is finally becoming aware of its responsibility and has begun to ask itself some questions: Whose earth is this? Do we have a right to throw away its treasures? Can a Christian be a NIMBY? What about Jesus' command to love our neighbors as ourselves? God requires justice; how do we excuse our trashing of poor nations?

Together, kids' activities and Christians' questions could change the course of the Great Trash Race. Imagine what would happen if these two forces combined — if Christian kids became active!

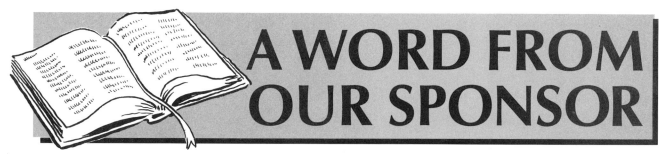

A WORD FROM OUR SPONSOR

Back to the Basics

Do you feel as if you're awash in a sea of gooey garbage, dripping dumps, and leaching landfills? Is your head swimming from the facts and figures ~~of the last two sections~~? Are you about to throw in the towel because the problem's too big? Do you wonder how you can be part of the solution? Then it's time to get this whole mess into some kind of order; time to get back to the basics, back to the very basics.

Genesis 1 is about as far back and as basic as we can get. It tells the story of God creating the earth. Every step of the way, it says that what God made was good. And just to be sure that we get the idea, at the end it declares everything *very* good. You can almost imagine God smiling at all those good things recently created.

Somewhere in this story of beginnings (Genesis 1:28 and 2:15, to be exact) God put people in charge of the whole business. Simply put, God made a very good world, put people in it, and told them to take care of it. But it still is God's world; we're just the caretakers.

That's it in a nutshell. If you forget the facts and figures about dripping dumps and leaching landfills, you can still remember what Genesis says: it's God's world, and we're supposed to take care of it. Obviously, trashing it doesn't fall under the general heading of "take care of it." Simple, right?

Actually, it becomes a little more complicated than that, ~~as you'll see when you read this section~~.

God talks a lot about justice in the Bible, and about taking care of the poor and helpless. This is all tied in with how we waste resources that others could use and throw away things that the poor never dream of owning. ~~If you think some of the stuff in this section has absolutely no relationship to the garbage glut, think again.~~

But basically, think of the world as God's and yourself as a caretaker. Then you'll be ready to roll up your sleeves rather than throw in the towel.

Twinkle, Twinkle

Twinkle, twinkle, Planet Earth
God made you and knows your worth.
He told us that we should care;
Keep you well, your treasures share.
Twinkle, twinkle, Planet Earth
God made you and knows your worth.

What Wood You Do?

According to certain experts:

☞ If all the wood and paper thrown away in the United States during one year were set aside and burned instead of dumped, it could heat 50 million homes for 20 years.

☞ Newsprint for Sunday newspapers alone uses 500,000 trees every week. That's a lot of wood.

☞ Almost a third of our household waste is packaging, and much of that is paper.

If you were in charge of Sunday newspapers, packaging, and heating homes for the poor, what wood you do? Is there anything that you *can* do?

IT'S YOUR TURN!

Whose Earth Is It?

Just who owns this earth? Unscramble the words below and place them in an order that makes sense.

earth world and everything in it, and the the the Lord's who live in it is all

_____ _____ _____

_____ _____ _____

_____ _____ _____

_____ _____ _____

_____ _____ _____

_____ _____

(Psalm 24:1, NIV)

Food for Thought

We're told that if all the people in the United States reduced the amount of meat they used (including what they threw away) by 10 percent yearly, the grain and soybeans used to feed that "meat" could instead feed 60 million people.

According to some experts, eight out of every hundred pounds of trash in the United States is food. That totals almost 13.7 million tons of food thrown away every year, they say.

Some experts claim that 18 people die of starvation every minute of every hour of every day. That's more than 9 million a year.

Others say that the number is closer to 6 million a year.

Different experts come up with different numbers, but those numbers always add up to one conclusion: Many Americans throw away a lot of food while many people are starving.

Doing Double Duty

Want to "kill two birds with one stone" in four steps? Save some things you're going to dump and give them away instead. Here's how.

1. Call a local hospital, jail, Salvation Army, Goodwill, or any combination of these. Ask them what donations they accept: Magazines? Jigsaw puzzles? Clothes (how about those too-small tennies)? Toys and games? Ask for specific suggestions and keep a list of what should go where.

2. Take paper grocery bags, write the list of suggestions on the outside of each bag, and put one next to each wastebasket in your house. Tell your family to throw those items into the bags rather than in the trash.

3. When the bags are full, sort them to

be sure that the items are usable. (No one wants tennies with holes in the soles or puzzles without all the pieces.) Weigh the good stuff to see how much "trash" you've saved.

4. Ask your parents to help you bring the stuff to the right places.

Points to Ponder

1. *Christian NIMBYs?* — If you've forgotten what a NIMBY is, reread "NIMBYs Edge Out TWABALs in Great Trash Race," Section Two. Then read what Christ says in Matthew 7:21, and what Paul says in Romans 13:9b, 10. Do you think a Christian can be a NIMBY?

2. *Un-Christian Trash or Christian Un-Trash?* Read Matthew 25:34-40; then read "Doing Double Duty," this section, if you haven't already done so. Are these two connected in any way? Is it un-Christian to trash certain things? Is there such a thing as Christian trash or maybe Christian un-trash?

Wheel of the Fortunate

The category for this puzzle is "What God Requires of Us."

The vowels are already in place. The consonants to be used are listed below. Put them in their proper places to solve the puzzle. The answer is found in Micah 6:8 (NIV).

```
_ O A _ _ _ U _ _ _ Y A _ _ _ O _ O _ E
_ E _ _ Y A _ _ _ O _ A _ _ _ U _ _ _ Y
_ I _ _ Y O U _ _ O _.
```

B, 2 C's, 3 D's, G, 2 H's, J, K, 4 L's, 2 M's, 2 N's, 2 R's, S, 6 T's, V, 2 W's

Driving the Point Home

If you've done double duty (see "Doing Double Duty," this section), expand your operations a bit. Try the same thing at school or at church. Organize some kind of drive.

You might want to zero in on just one thing to collect at first, maybe clothes or magazines. Explain to your classmates (or Sunday School class, or other church group) why you are doing this. Be sure to report back to them how many pounds of their "trash" you saved for others to use.

What Next?

Do you still feel as if you're awash in a sea, only now it's a sea of garbage and starvation, waste and want, and careless caretaking? Do you think that Christians, especially, should watch their waste lines and share some of Creation's treasures? Are you completely baffled about how and where to start?

Well, buck up; that's the way it should be at this stage of the game.

By this time you definitely should be aware of the garbage glut, how we're trashing Creation and wasting God's gifts. And you should want to do something about it, but probably are wondering just where to start.

The rest of *Trash Can Review* is about just where to start. So start reading Section Four and work your way to the end. By then you should be well on your way to taking care of Creation better and sharing more by reducing your personal waste line.

Just Say No

Our trash problem is a lot like a kid's messy bedroom. It's almost impossible to clean up, yet we know we have to do something about it. The mess is unsightly and — in the case of trash, not your bedroom — very often unhealthy, unfair, and un-Christian. So where do we start?

Has an adult ever told you that, if you had put your playthings away (or hung up your clothes) as soon as you were finished with them, you wouldn't have had the mess in the first place? In other words, don't start the mess and you won't have one to clean up. Well, the same advice applies to trash.

Adults are starting to catch on to their own advice. They're realizing that we're better off just not making so much trash. In other words, just say no to trash, refuse the refuse, don't throw things away. Adults often call this "source reduction." The source is you; you are supposed to reduce your own amount of trash.

This doesn't mean that you simply let your trash pile up and refuse to throw it away. Imagine the mess in your bedroom if you did that!

Source reduction means that you refuse to accept things that will soon become trash. If you don't have it, you can't throw it away.

A great place to start is with packaging — all the paper, cardboard, and plastic that surrounds the stuff you buy. Also all the boxes, bags, and wrappings that the paper, cardboard, and plastic

are put into when you buy them. The only thing you do with them is cart them home and throw them away.

Another easy target is disposables — tissues, juice boxes, straws, and so on. Can you imagine things made to be used once and then thrown away? What a waste of resources and a bunch of trash! That's exactly what disposables are.

Saying no to trash — reducing it at the source — is a lot like keeping your bedroom neat. Don't mess it up in the first place, and you won't have much of a problem.

Actually, it's better than keeping your bedroom neat.

When you say no to trash, you say no to wasting the resources used to make that trash. Maybe then those resources might be used to heat homes or clothe the poor or feed the hungry. You're treating God's gifts, God's people, and God's earth with more respect.

A Wrap Rap

A problem with our rubbish is we throw a lot of wraps;
  There's tissue, plastic bubbles, bags, and boxes with their flaps,
Containers, crates, and bottles with those crazy kid-proof caps.
  We bottle, box, and bag it, and then wrap it with more wraps!

Candies are just dandy, but we wrap them oh so tight;
  The outer bag is plastic and to open it's a fright.
Then we hit the cellophane and tug with all our might,
  To find beneath that wrapping yet another — what a sight!

A game sold in a box alone? Impossible to find!
  Around the box is plastic wrap, the thin and crinkly kind.
And in the box, around each piece, some tissue to unwind.
  A tiny game, a great big box; it simply blows my mind!

That single size of juice or food, or packages of sugar?
  More paper there than nourishment is all that I can figure.
So what's the point? I thought and thought, and said, "Well, I'll be jiggered.
  I think they wrap the products thus to make them look much bigger!"

I cannot wear new tennies home to cover up my socks.
  They must be wrapped in tissue, then be put inside a box,
And then inside a plastic bag to carry a few blocks.
  A pox on all that packaging! A pox, I say, a POX!

We're gagging on our garbage and I know one reason why;
  There's far too many wrappings put on everything we buy.
The purchases are tiny things; the wrappings pile high.
  Who pays for all that packaging? We both do, you and I!

It's time to stop this nonsense and to give our earth a break,
  Reduce the trail of wrappings that we each leave in our wake.
Forget the box, forget the bag, cut out that trash we make,
  And keep the earth a cleaner place for everybody's sake.

Bright Ideas

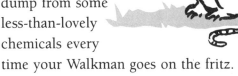

1. *Save a Bag.* When you go shopping at a mall, buy your biggest item first. Let the clerk put it in a large bag. Add any other items you buy to that first bag rather than accepting a bag for each item.

2. *Cash for Trash?* Refuse to buy toys and games that look as if they'll fall apart after a few uses. You may pay more for a sturdy game, but you'll have it a lot longer, and you'll keep it out of the dumps.

3. *Charge It.* Refuse to buy "disposable" batteries. Insist on the rechargeable kind whenever possible. (Of course, you'll need a battery charger, too.) Rechargeables can be used over and over and over. . . . They cost more, but you save money in the long run. Besides that, you'll spare a dump from some less-than-lovely chemicals every time your Walkman goes on the fritz.

4. *Refuse the Refuse.* Refuse to buy anything that comes in too much packaging. Simply refuse. If you can, tell a clerk why you won't buy it. If enough of us refuse, packaging people will get the message.

Popcorn Packaging

Foam peanuts used when shipping breakable goods may soon be a thing of the past. As an increasing number of manufacturers realize that their packaging simply clogs landfills, they are switching to more "earth friendly" fillers.

Some companies now shred newspapers and use that as packing. This gives second life to the paper, and puts something more degradable into the trash.

A few inventive companies are now packing in popcorn; popped, that is, without butter. They say that their new packing is cheap, lightweight, plentiful, and even edible. Now all we need is a tasty box!

Disposing of Disposables

If we can't throw things away because there is no "away," then we also can't dispose of disposables. A disposable is something that's made to be used once and then thrown away. But we can't really throw it away, so it isn't really disposable. Yet, in the course of one year, Americans throw out 18 billion "disposable" diapers, 2 billion "disposable" razors, 2.5 billion "disposable" batteries, 2.2 billion "disposable" pens, 500 million "disposable" lighters, and 2 million "disposable" cameras.

Unpackaging Popcorn

Smart shoppers are sending manufacturers messages they cannot ignore. In an effort to reduce their trash, these (non)-consumers are refusing to accept excess packaging. They simply leave it at the store.

Here's an example. A person picks a package of microwave popcorn from the shelf and takes it to the cashier to pay for it. Before forking over the money the customer says, "I don't need all this extra packaging. Do you mind if I leave it here?" Then he or she opens the box, takes out the three popcorn bags, and takes the extra wrappings off them. "This is all I need," the customer says, holding up the three bags. The store is left with the box and the cellophane wrappings that went around the individual bags.

If all customers simply refused excess packaging, manufacturers would get the message in a hurry!

Want to avoid the whole mess, at least with popcorn? Buy it in a glass jar and recycle the jar. (See Section Six.)

IT'S YOUR TURN

Sorting It Out

Circle all the wrappings you find in the trash. Put an X through the "disposables."

Bag It

Even the most careful customers sometimes must walk out of a store with a bag in tow. Nowadays the array of bags at the end of a checkout line can boggle anybody's mind. What's the best kind to use? That's a personal decision, but it helps to know the facts.

Brown paper bags are actually more polluting to make than are plastic bags. They also take a long time to degrade (break down) in a modern landfill. But plastic bags may never break down.

Yet plastic bags don't take up as much room in a dump as do paper bags.

Paper bags are biodegradable; bacteria will help them degrade, eventually. Some plastic bags are supposed to be biodegradable, but experts claim that this has been proved only in labs and may not work in dumps.

Some plastic is photodegradable; it breaks down after it has been exposed to sunlight. Yet the bag that goes from store to bus to home to trash can may never be exposed to direct sunlight.

Confusing, isn't it? It's still best to avoid the confusion and carry your own cloth bag.

IT'S YOUR TURN

You Name It

Name five different things made to be thrown away after one use.

1. _____
2. _____
3. _____
4. _____
5. _____

The Great Paper Chase

Here are four simple things you can do immediately to reduce your trash and save some trees.

1. Refuse to use paper tissues; use cloth hankies instead.

2. Refuse to use paper towels; use a cloth one instead.

3. Refuse to use paper napkins; use a cloth one instead.

4. Refuse to use only one side of a paper; use both sides instead.

Show and Tell

Having trouble convincing adults in your house to refuse paper and reuse cloth? Then try the following grown-up version of Show and Tell.

Go through your family's trash the night before it's hauled away. Take out all the paper towels, paper napkins, tissues, and papers with writing on only one side. Use gloves to avoid germy hands. Put all those paper products into one bag (maybe you'll need more than one), take a long look, and then show them to the rest of your family. That's the amount of trash your family could have saved.

If that doesn't convince your family, save your show-and-tell material for a month; you should have an impressive mess by that time.

The Impossible Dream?

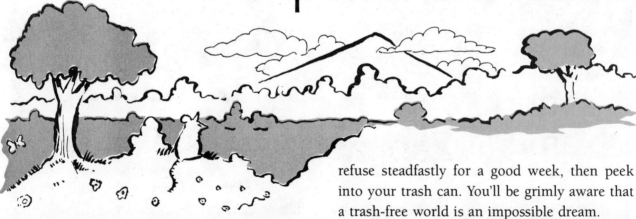

So now you're all geared up to share and save Creation. Just say no to trash, especially all that extra packaging and those disposables; your trash can will magically empty and you'll help save resources, right? Well, sort of; but sort of not, too.

Refusing the refuse is a good start, probably the best start we can make. But the world isn't perfect; there will always be trash. Refuse the refuse steadfastly for a good week, then peek into your trash can. You'll be grimly aware that a trash-free world is an impossible dream.

But "impossible" doesn't mean we stop trying. To buck up your spirits a bit, think about how much more trash there would have been and how many more resources would have been used if you hadn't tried at all.

Besides that, there are other things we can do. Read on for more ideas. And keep on dreaming of a cleaner Creation, with resources wisely shared. That's not impossible.

TREASURES IN YOUR TRASH

Score One for the Pack Rats

There was a time not too long ago — you might remember it — when people who saved things were considered a little odd, if not downright strange. A kid who was proud of old tennies was not quite normal. Someone who used a hand-me-down bike wouldn't advertise the fact. And woe be to anyone who actually kept "junk." That person was called a pack rat; the term was *not* a compliment.

But times have changed, and kids have changed with the times. Nowadays, saving things isn't considered weird at all. In fact, if you can reuse something, you're considered quite clever. And the more you can reuse things, or remake them for another use, or give them away for someone else to use, the more clever you're considered to be.

It all makes sense, of course. The more things you reuse, the fewer things you throw away. The fewer things you throw away, the less trash you have and the less you waste God's precious gifts.

That's the second line of defense against waste and the garbage glut: reuse anything you can. Score one for the pack rats, and read the rest of this section for their tips and tidbits.

Zappable Wraps

Many people are eyeing the bags and boxes they tote home from the grocery store with their microwave in mind. Are the wraps zappable? Then they can be reused.

Crinkly cellophane and boxes don't work well. Cellophane tears too easily, and it's hard to stuff new food into old boxes.

Breadbags and bakery bags work well for a reheat. Simply slip the food into the bag and give it a quick zap. You've saved a piece of wax paper (or plastic wrap, or a paper napkin) and you've reused a bag.

Some deli foods come in containers with lids. If they can be zapped once with the original foods in them, the containers can be zapped again and again with leftovers. That's reusing food and the wraps.

An extra tip: Wax paper is a good zappable wrap, because it can be reused. Plastic wrap usually gives up after one zap.

Bright Ideas

IT'S YOUR TURN

1. *That Old Bag.* Snare an empty bag from the trash. (A plastic bag works well for this.) Clean it, dry it, and then shove it to the bottom of your book bag. If you buy anything on the way home from school, you'll have a reusable bag with you. You can kill two birds with one stone; reuse an old bag while you refuse a new one.

2. *Box Lunches.* Take your lunch to school in a lunch box that you can use all year. Take your liquids in a thermos or plastic juice container. Stuff the sandwiches into used breadwrappers, or reuse wax paper. See how many times you can use the same breadwrapper or piece of wax paper.

3. *Instant Replay.* Got any old books you know by heart, puzzles you can do with your eyes shut, or games that bore you? Give them a second chance by swapping with a friend. You can always trade back later.

4. *Counting the Cost.* Find a special spot in your bedroom to keep a paper bag. Take it along when you go from home to a store. Every time you reuse that bag at a store, leave the receipt in the bottom. When the bag wears out, you can tell how many times you've used it by how many receipts are in it.

5. *Sharing the Wealth.* Put an empty box or bag "for the needy" in your garage or basement. Tell your family it's there for donations of clothes, toys, games, etc. When it's full, put the stuff in order and take it to a place like Salvation Army.

6. *Foiled Again.* You can use old aluminum foil over and over again. Wrap pieces of a puzzle in it, keep your pencils and pens together in your book bag, keep your treasures from your junk drawer sorted with it, etc., etc. Old pie tins work well for feeding a pet (but not goldfish!); they can also hold birdseed for your wild feathered friends. A divided aluminum dish is great for keeping your desk drawers neat.

7. *Good News.* Wrap a present in newspaper. You can hint at what's inside by the section you use — comics for a gag gift, sports news for a baseball mitt, clothing ads for a T-shirt, etc., etc. Use a marker or crayon to draw a ribbon and bow.

8. *Articles of Interest.* Got a bunch of old magazines you're finished with? Hospitals love them for waiting rooms. News magazines tend to go out-of-date quickly, but other magazines are just fine.

9. *Yardage Sale.* Stow away a few paper grocery sacks in a corner of your closet. Throw outgrown clothes, memorized books, and "boring" games into them. When they're full, hold a Yardage Sale. (That's a combination of a garage and a yard sale, so you can have it either place, or both places.) Invite your friends to sell with you.

Your Ideas

Use this space. Please don't waste it.
List any ideas you or your classmates
may have for reusing things.

_____

_____

_____

_____

_____

_____

_____

_____

New Life for Old Duds

Got a sweater that you don't wear anymore? Tennies that just don't make it? Jeans that don't reach your ankles? Thinking of tossing them out? Don't be so hasty; there are lots of things you can do with them.

Salvation Army and Goodwill Industries take used clothing to give (or sell at a low price) to people who need them. But, they say, the clothes must be good. A sweater with holes in it can't keep anyone warm. A pair of tennies too dirty to be cleaned will give anyone the yucks. Good candidates for a second time around are clothes that are too small or don't match or that simply sit in the closet.

Worn-out clothes usually can find new life in a new form. Sweats, T-shirts, and even socks make great dust rags. Shirts and blouses can come back as cloth napkins and handkerchiefs. Old jeans are great cutoffs for warm weather. Old bath towels work well for drying cars or bikes left out in the rain. They can also be trimmed down and moved to the kitchen to replace paper towels in cleaning up spills.

Does anybody you know make baby clothes? Doll clothes? Just plain smaller clothes for smaller kids? Need rags for washing the dog? Did you ever think of dyeing something that's the wrong color? Or combining two old pieces of clothing to make one new one? Got the idea? Don't dump those duds, dude. There's probably plenty of life left in them.

IT'S YOUR TURN

Twice as Nice

List at least two ways you can reuse the items pictured below.

Golden Oldies

NOT TOO LONG AGO. . . .

- Kids used only one pen per student through a whole year at school. When the pen ran out of ink it could be refilled. (Ink came in glass bottles, which now can be recycled; see "Cullet — Anything but Trash," Section Six.) The pens were called fountain pens and were slightly different from the ballpoints we throw away today.

- Students carried their lunches to school in reusable, metal lunch boxes. They took their own milk or juice, usually in a reusable thermos designed to keep drinks cold or hot. Their milk at home came in glass bottles that were returned for refilling.

- Sandwiches in lunch boxes were usually wrapped with wax paper rather than plastic wrap. Special treats like pieces of pie had their own reusable, wedge-shaped containers. Kids slicked out the containers, brushed the crumbs off the paper, and took it all back home inside the lunch box.

- Church fellowship dinners and school lunches were served on ceramic plates with real glass glasses. True, someone had to wash the dishes; but that was part of the "fellowship," and there was much less trash.

- Nobody "flicked a Bic." The lighters they used for candles, grills, and fireplaces could be refilled when they ran out of fuel.

- People didn't throw razors away, only the blades. They could open the top of the razor, take out the old blade, and put in a new one. There were small slits in the back of bathroom medicine cabinets; old razor blades were thrown into the slit and buried in the wall.

- Kids grew out of their clothes rather than wear them out. Parents patched torn clothes, darned socks, and put new soles on shoes until the kids were too big for the clothes. Small clothes were passed on to younger brothers and sisters.

- Books were treasures never to be trashed. Readers swapped the books they had finished. If all else failed, they set the books aside for the next garage sale. Old Bibles were mended and sent to missionaries for distribution.

- Trash was put in metal pails rather than plastic bags, and there was a lot less of it.

You don't remember any of this? Ask your parents about it. If they don't remember, ask Grandma or Grandpa.

Cash for Trash

Garage sales are back in style. Why? Because they're a great way to cut down on trash, save resources, make a little cash, and spread the wealth, all in one fell swoop. Everybody wins at a garage sale.

Whoever sells the stuff makes out like a bandit. They get cash for their "trash." And they cut down on their trash to boot.

Buyers win, too. They get things at ridiculously low prices. Sometimes they get things they could not otherwise afford.

Even Creation wins. Reusing old rather than buying new saves precious resources. And fewer items bite the dust and clog the landfills.

IT'S YOUR TURN

Flashback!

Remember the five disposable items you listed in the last section? (If not, go back and check.) Now, list five reusable things you can use instead of those five disposables.

1. _____

2. _____

3. _____

4. _____

5. _____

IT'S YOUR TURN

Scavenger Hunt

Go through your trash can and pick out the items listed below. Score seven points or less on this one and you're a super pack rat. Score more and you qualify as a scavenger.

Item	Points	Number found	Total
Brown paper bags	2	x _____	= _____
A breadwrapper	2	x _____	= _____
A plastic bag that is not a breadwrapper	2	x _____	= _____
A newspaper	1	x _____	= _____
A piece of tinfoil	1	x _____	= _____
An aluminum pie plate or food dish	3	x _____	= _____
A fast food or deli container with an attached top	3	x _____	= _____
A piece of old clothing	5	x _____	= _____
		Grand Tally	_____

Your Scavenger Hunt Findings

Now check this section to see how you can reuse each of the items listed that you found in your trash. Each item is mentioned at least once.

_____   _____

_____   _____

_____   _____

_____   _____

_____   _____

_____   _____

_____   _____

_____   _____

_____   _____

_____   _____

_____   _____

_____   _____

Your Talking Trash Can

Enough already! You've got the point, right? Right! But just in case, let's go over this one more time. You can reuse lots of stuff rather than throw it away. Your trash can may be alive with possibilities; so alive you can almost hear it talk.

"Take me as I am and use me again." Listen to those bags and boxes and extra wrappings you tried to toss. They've worked for you only once; they're begging to work for you again and again.

"Save me; give me a new home!" Is that something you've outgrown? Those too-tight tennies? Maybe a game that's too young for you? You loved it once and now you're going to throw it away? Give it away instead, and everyone will be happier.

"I know how to make you rich!" Some piece of "trash" may be exaggerating a bit, but not too much. That old bike that's been in the corner since you got a new one, that Walkman you abandoned in favor of a boom box, the skateboard you never use — someone may be itching to get his or her hands on those things. They may even pay you for them!

"I'll change, I'll change. Just keep me and see!" That could be almost anything begging for a second chance at life; a newspaper longing to wrap itself around a gift, jeans willing to double as cutoffs, or even an egg carton with dreams of becoming an art project.

"Whtzz mph compt quii!" What's that, you don't understand it? Neither do we, but that's the whole point. Use your imagination and you may hear all sorts of things pleading to be used again and again.

Who knows? You may have the makings of a good pack rat!

Right On, Solomon

Long ago, Solomon said that there was nothing new under the sun. In fact, he followed that by saying, "Is there anything of which one can say, 'Look! This is something new'? It was here already, long ago; it was here before our time."

He wasn't talking about our trash. Nor was he talking about recycling; but it surely can make you think in those terms. It almost makes you wonder if Solomon, way back then, knew that Creation is one big recycler. It is, you know.

Take that oak tree in your back yard. The acorn that started the oak came from another oak tree, which came from an acorn, which came from another oak tree, which came from an acorn, etc., etc., etc., all the way down to the very first oak tree or acorn, whichever came first. The sun that helped it grow has been around as long as the earth. So has the earth in which it's growing. And everybody knows that rain has been recycled since the beginning of time. The whole business has been here forever; it's just changed form.

Hold it! What about something like your skateboard? Solomon didn't have a skateboard.

Of course not, but think about its parts. They all came, in some form, from the earth. Even the plastic parts (Solomon didn't have plastic, either) came from petroleum, which came from old dead things in the ground. Those things, originally live, came from other living

things that came from other living things, which came from other living things, etc., etc., etc., to the beginning of time.

You get the idea: There is nothing new under the sun; it's all recycled. Solomon may not have been thinking in those terms, but he was right on. Now it's time for us to latch right on to that idea and give recycling a boost.

If you haven't said no to it, and you can't reuse it, maybe you can recycle it. Read this section for all sorts of hints on recycling.

Bright Ideas

1. *No Place like Home.* If your family does not recycle, get them started. Put bags or boxes next to your wastebaskets and tell all members to toss their recyclables in there. When the bags are full, sort them into separate bags (one for glass, one for aluminum, etc.) and store those bags in the garage or basement. When you have a good-sized load, ask an adult to help you take it to a recycling center.

2. *Try the Can-Can.* Once you've got the hang of recycling your own cans, branch out a bit. Offer to take in your friends' and neighbors' cans. Set up a "can barrel" in your lunchroom at school and the fellowship room at church. Pick up stray cans. Patrol those pizza parties for pop cans. If you have a deposit law, take the ones with prices on their heads to a refund center and you will be amply rewarded. Of course, you'll recycle the rest.

3. *Patrol That Paper.* Newspaper drives are not news. They've been around for a long time. If your school doesn't hold them, maybe you can get one started. And you can convince your school to recycle other paper. Find out from local recyclers what kinds of paper they accept. Write the list of "acceptables" on boxes and put the boxes next to wastebaskets, with instructions to put all recyclable paper in the box. Many paper recyclers will pick up your load and supply you with a list of just how many trees you have saved.

4. *Share the Wealth.* Take any cold hard cash that you earn from recycling and give it to a worthy cause. That way you'll really be sharing God's gifts, both the resources you save and the extras you earn.

Fun Facts

According to some authorities:

1. Recycling one ton of paper saves 17 trees.

2. Recycled newspapers come back as more newspapers, cereal boxes, egg cartons, animal bedding, construction paper, even cat litter.

3. Other recycled paper returns as game boards, jigsaw puzzles, gift boxes, book covers, show tickets, etc., etc.

4. Approximately one-third of all U.S. household trash could be recycled.

5. Many schools and offices recycle. Does yours? People then bring their paper from home to be recycled. Good idea!

A Price on Their Heads

Don't go out and dump everything into a recycle bin — yet. First, find out whether some bottles and cans have a price on their heads.

If you have a deposit law in your area, you can get cold cash for beverage containers — that's basically pop and beer bottles and cans. Someone paid 5 or 10 cents per container when they were full. You can return the empties and get that deposit. The empties are recycled, so no one's losing out on that end.

Every deposit law and every return center play by slightly different rules. For example, many places won't take stomped-on cans (See "The Three-step Stomp," this section). So, before you stomp or dump into a bin, check on the rules in your area. You may find it very rewarding.

The Three-step Stomp

What's the best way to get your cans ready for recycling? Do the three-step stomp:

1. Rinse out the can (so you don't splatter leftovers all over the floor).
2. Take off the label and both ends.
3. Stomp on the middle.

That way, your cans take less space and won't roll out of the bag or whatever you put them in. Throw the ends in too, but watch those sharp edges.

Want to separate aluminum cans from other metals? If you don't know which is which, use a magnet. If the can doesn't stick, it's aluminum; if it does, it's another metal.

The Plastics Puzzle

Puzzled about whether and how to recycle what plastics? Most people are. Information on recycling plastics changes continually. However, here are a few general things you should know.

If it's plastic and it has held food, by law it may not be recycled to hold food again. So your plastic pop bottles, styrofoam food trays, coffee cups, etc., will probably do a one-round recycling trip. They'll be shredded or melted and come back as garbage cans, fence posts, plastic "lumber," flower pots, fiberfill, and lots of other ingenious things. But that's about it for their bag of tricks. The next time around, they usually hit the trash can.

The variety of plastics used for bottles can boggle the mind. To help keep you sane, the plastics industry is beginning to label the stuff. If you look at the bottom of the bottle, you may see a recycle logo with a number inside. The number refers to the kind of plastic that bottle is made from. As a rule of thumb, the lower the number, the more recyclable the bottle. Ones through threes have a good chance at a second life. Fours through sevens are very "iffy" at this point. Recycling them is very difficult.

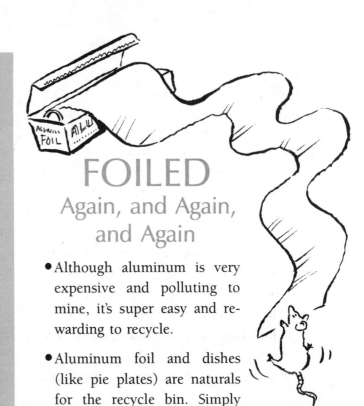

FOILED
Again, and Again, and Again

- Although aluminum is very expensive and polluting to mine, it's super easy and rewarding to recycle.

- Aluminum foil and dishes (like pie plates) are naturals for the recycle bin. Simply clean them and dump them in.

- Recycling one aluminum can (instead of making one new one) saves enough energy to keep your TV running for three hours.

- The can you recycle on New Year's Day may be back on the shelf by Valentine's Day. It may make two round trips during summer vacation.

- The energy saved by recycling aluminum cans in 1988 could have supplied enough electrical power for the residents of New York City for six months.

- Throwing an aluminum can away is like filling that can half full of gasoline and dumping that out on the ground. (That much energy is lost.)

- According to Recycle America, if 250 people recycled an aluminum can every day (or if *you* recycled 250 cans a day!) for a year, the energy saved would be equal to the energy in 1,750 to 3,500 gallons of gas. That's a fill-up for a small car once a week for 3½ to 7 years.

It's a No-No

Generally speaking, things that are made from a mixture of materials can't be recycled. Here's a list to start you thinking in the right direction. If you can't figure out a way to reuse these things, maybe you'd better refuse them.

1. *Aerosol cans* are made of several metals and some plastics. These cans also tend to blow up in incinerators — not good! Look for pump bottles rather than aerosol cans.

2. *Juice boxes* have cardboard, aluminum, and plastic all molded together and are good for nothing but your trash can. Returnable or recyclable cans or bottles are a much better choice.

3. *Squeezable plastic bottles* like those for ketchup, mustard, and honey are made from several types of plastic. In combination, they can't be easily recycled. Better to search for glass bottles.

4. *Stickers* are too sticky on the back side; they gum up the works.

5. *Wax paper*, obviously, is wax and paper. But you can reuse it.

Cullet— Anything but Trash

Most glass doesn't ever have to hit the trash can. It can be recycled over and over and over. Old broken glass, called cullet, is simply added to new molten glass and shaped into almost anything. Because cullet melts at a lower temperature than the ingredients of new glass, recycling glass saves energy as well as trash space.

A few glass things don't qualify. Light bulbs, ceramic glass, dishes, and plate glass contain "extras" not found in bottle glass, and can't be recycled. But jars and bottles definitely can.

To recycle glass, simply clean it and separate according to color — clear, brown, or green. (When in doubt, guess.) You don't even have to take the label off, because that will vaporize when the cullet is heated.

IT'S YOUR TURN

Quickie Quiz

(All the answers are in this section)

1. List two materials that can be recycled again and again and again.

1._____

2._____

2. List the three steps in the Three-step Stomp.

1._____

2._____

3._____

3. What kinds of things, generally, cannot be recycled?

_____

_____

Look for the Logo

Wonder if something is recycled or recyclable? Look for this logo.

Then read the fine print nearby. Usually it will tell you whether the item is made from recycled materials and whether it can be recycled. This logo is popping up on more and more things.

Sneak a Peek

Did you ever wonder about the former life of your cereal box — what it was before it became that box on your breakfast table? Probably not. But just in case, there's an easy way to find out. Sneak a peek at the inside of the box.

If the inside is grey as a rainy day, that box is recycled paper. In its former life it may have been the sports page in a newspaper, or a private office memo. If the inside of your box is white, it is not recycled paper. In its former life, that cereal box was a living tree.

Closing the Logo Loop

The recycle logo loop suggests, of course, that a thing can be used over and over and over again. That's true, with one big IF . . .

IF the recycled thing, whatever it is, is used again. Everyone in the world can bring newspapers to be recycled, but if no one will use recycled paper we'd be stuck.

IF you're a sincere recycler, you'll pick up both ends of the loop. You'll bring things to be recycled, and you'll try to buy things that are recycled. Look for that loopy logo and try to buy recycled.

Sorting It Out

Circle all the things that you think can be recycled.

Recycle Address Book

Check to see whether the items listed below can be recycled in your area. If you can, list the location nearest you that accepts each item.

Plastic bottles _____

Plastic bags _____

Newspapers _____

Glass _____

Metal _____

Aluminum _____

Styrofoam_____

Cardboard _____

Appliances _____

Other _____

The End of
the Line

You can see from the size of this section that there is a lot to recycling, and there's a lot of stuff to recycle. Just how much, just what, and just how depend on the area in which you live.

Different communities recycle in different ways. Some people can put the stuff near the curb for pickup. Others have to haul it to a recycling center. Still others may have to search high and low for a recycling center. If you're in the last group, pressure your politicians to start a recycling program. Remind them that you're a future voter.

Different recyclers take different things.

The big three are usually glass, newspapers, and metals (especially aluminum). Some will take plastics, some will take other paper, and a few places even take old appliances (just in case you have a stove you want to get rid of!). It's up to you to find out what the recycler in your area takes.

Then it's up to you to recycle as much as you can. Because that's the end of the line. Anything still left in your trash can will probably stay there. At least until the trash is picked up. And you know what happens to it after that.

YOUR TRASH CAN REVIEW

R You Ready for This?

We've touched on nearly everything we know at this point, about how to avoid trashing Creation and wasting its treasures. We've reached the end of the line . . . almost.

Just in case you feel confused or a bit overwhelmed yet, this section should help. It's basically review, designed to tie things up into one neat package, if that's possible.

If we could condense Sections Four, Five, and Six into only three words, those words would be *reduce, reuse,* and *recycle.* People often call that the three R's of solid waste management.

Reduce the amount of trash you make. That's best done by simply saying "no"; by refusing to buy or use things that will end up in the trash soon. If you don't take trash in, you won't throw it out. And you'll save the resources used in making that trash. Saving resources is the first step toward sharing them.

Reuse whatever you can. Once you have it, use it again and again and again. Then reuse it again and again and again. Then change it, give it away, sell it; do whatever you can to prolong its life. Every time you reuse something, you avoid the waste that goes along with making something new, and you avoid glutting your garbage pail.

Recycle whatever you can. When you finally have to dump it, throw it into a recycle bin. Of course, you've got to think about that before you get it. Buy recyclable stuff; recycled recyclable stuff is better yet. Be part of the never-ending recycle loop, and you'll have less trash and use fewer resources.

That's it in a nutshell. Keep the three R's in mind, review this Review, and you're on your way to reducing your waste line.

It's Earthcare Jeopardy

Each phrase answers the question, "What is (are) _____ ?"
All the answers are in this book. See how many you know without looking
them up. A perfect score is 3,000 points.

POINTS	REDUCE	REUSE	RECYCLE
100	Things made to be used once and then thrown away.	Hospitals like these for their waiting rooms.	Broken glass, gathered for remelting.
	_____	_____	_____
200	What we can say to over-packaged goods.	Cutoffs, napkins, dust rags, etc.	Very expensive to mine, yet easy to recycle.
	_____	_____	_____
300	The number of homes that our discarded paper and wood could heat for 20 years.	Salvation Army, Goodwill Industries, etc.	The number of trees saved when one ton of paper is recycled.
	_____	_____	_____
400	An alternative to a disposable battery.	An event at which trash is reduced, and wealth is spread.	Aerosol cans, juice boxes, and plastic squeeze bottles.
	_____	_____	_____

(Answer key on page 63)

Instant Recall

The three R's of reducing your waste line are:

R_____   R_____   R_____

Sorting It Out

Here's your old friend, the trash can, one more time. Put an X through all the trash you never needed in the first place. Circle the stuff you could reuse by changing it. Put a box around everything that you can recycle.

Review Your Trash Can

Remember when you weighed your trash at the beginning of this review? Here's your chance to see how much progress you've made. Do it again, and compare the results. Check Section One to see exactly what to do and how you fared the first time

DATE: _____

MY PERSONAL TRASH WEIGHED _____ POUNDS.

The End of the Matter

Obviously, this is the end of your *Trash Can Review*. But it's really only the beginning of reviewing your trash can. Remember the three R's and you're on your way. You'll find that keeping your trash in check becomes easier with practice.

Besides that, as more people begin to do something about the problem, there should be more ways for you to pitch in. Soon you should be able to buy more stuff in less packaging. More people will have more ideas on how to reuse stuff. And more recycle centers (not to mention recyclable and recycled things) should pop up all over the place.

Information and technology in this field change almost daily. Keep your eyes and ears open for new developments. This can become very confusing. Whom to believe? How to proceed? How to keep up with the changes?

The best way to do that is to stick to the basics and work from there. Start with the one fact that never changes: God wants us to care for Creation and share its treasures. That's where we begin. And, as you guessed, there never will be an end to this matter.

Books You Can Read

Below is a list of books on the environment. Most of these titles can be found in your local bookstore or library.

Bodies of Water: Fun, Facts, and Activities, by Caroline Arnold (Franklin Watts, 387 Park Ave. S., New York, NY 10016; 212-686-7070, 800-843-3749. 1985; not in print)

Chadwick the Crab, by Priscilla Cummings (Tidewater Publishers, Box 456, Centreville, MD 21617; 301-758-1075. 1986; $5.95)

Endangered Animals, by National Wildlife Federation (Ranger Rick Books, 1400 16th St. N.W., Washington, DC 20036; 202-797-6800. 1989; $19.95)

50 Simple Things Kids Can Do to Save the Earth, by The Earth Works Group (Andrews & McMeel, 4900 Main St., Kansas City, MO 64112; 800-826-4216. 1990; $7.95)

Going Green: A Kid's Handbook to Saving the Environment, by John Elkington and others (Puffin Books, 375 Hudson St., New York, NY 10014; 901-627-2521. 1990; $8.95)

It's Your Environment: Things to Think About, Things to Do, by the Environmental Action Coalition (Charles Scribner's Sons, Front and Brown Sts., Riverside, NJ 08075; 800-257-8247. 1971; not in print)

Just A Dream, by Chris Van Allsburg (Houghton Mifflin Co. 1 Beacon St. Boston, MA 02108; 800-225-3362, 1990; $17.95)

Keepers of the Earth, by Michael J. Caduto and Joseph Bruchac (Fulcrun, Inc., 350 Indiana St., Suite 510, Golden, CO 80401; 303-277-1623, 800-992-2908. 1989; $19.95)

The Kids Nature Book: 365 Indoor/Outdoor Activities, by Susan Milord (Williamson Publishing, Church Hill Rd., Charlotte, VT 05445; 802-425-2102, 800-234-8791. 1989; $12.95)

The Lorax, by Dr. Seuss (Random House, 201 E. 50th St., New York, NY 10022; 212-751-2600. 1971; $10.95)

Nature for the Very Young, by Marcia Bowden (John Wiley and Sons, 605 Third Ave., New York, NY 10158; 212-850-6276. 1989; $10.95)

The Ocean Book, by The Center for Environmental Education (John Wiley and Sons, 605 Third Ave., New York, NY 10158; 212-850-6276. 1989; $11.95)

Planet Earth series: *The Oceans, Coastlines, Water on the Land, The Work of the Wind,* and *Weather and Climate,* by various authors (The Bookwright Press, 387 Park Ave. S., New York, NY 10016; 212-686-7070, 800-843-3749. 1988; not in print)

The Planet of Trash: An Environmental Fable, by George Poppel (National Press Inc., 7201

Wisconsin Ave., Suite 720, Bethesda, MD 20814; 301-657-1616. 1987; $9.95)

Poisoned Land: The Problem of Hazardous Waste, by Irene Kiefer (Atheneum, Macmillan Publishing Co., 866 Third Ave., New York, NY 10022; 800-257-8247. 1981; $13.95)

Professor Noah's Spaceship, by Brian Wildsmith (Oxford University Press, 200 Madison Ave., New York, NY 10016; 212-679-7300. 1987; $4.95)

Project Ecology book series: *Air Ecology, Animal Ecology, Urban Ecology,* and *Water Ecology,* by Jennifer Cochrane (The Bookwright Press, 387 Park Ave. S., New York, NY 10016; 212-686-7070, 800-843-3749. 1988; not in print)

Save the Earth! An Ecology Handbook for Kids, by Betty Miles (Alfred A. Knopf Inc., 201 E. 50th St. New York, NY 10022; 800-638-6460)

Sierra Club Summer Book, by Linda Allison (Sierra Club Books, 730 Polk St., San Francisco, CA 94109; 415-776-2211. 1989; $7.95)

Sierra Club Wayfinding Book, by Vicki McVey (Sierra Club Books, 730 Polk St., San Francisco, CA 94109; 415-776-2211. 1990; $13.95)

Weather Watch, by Valery Wyatt (Addison Wesley Publishing Company, Inc., Jacob Way, Reading, MA 01867; 617-944-3700. 1990; $8.95)

The Wump World, by Bill Peet (Houghton Mifflin Co., 1 Beacon St., Boston, MA 02108; 800-225-3362. 1974; $3.95)

Organizations You Can Contact

Below is a selection of organizations that offer information on the environment.

CENTER FOR MARINE CONSERVATION (1725 DeSales St. N.W., Suite 500, Washington, DC 20036; 202-429-5609) offers free coloring books, posters, and pamphlets on such sea creatures as sea turtles, dolphins, and whales.

COUSTEAU SOCIETY (870 Greenbrier Circle, Norfolk, VA 23517; 804-523-9335) offers family memberships for $28 that include *The Dolphin Log* for children and *The Calypso Log* for adults.

DEFENDERS OF WILDLIFE (1244 19th St. N.W., Washington, DC 20036; 202-659-9510) offers free pamphlets on endangered species and fact sheets on wild animals.

IZAAK WALTON LEAGUE OF AMERICA (1401 W. Blvd., Level B, Arlington, VA 22209; 703-528-1818) offers an S.O.S. (Save Our Streams) kit for $8 that includes a subscription to *Splash,* bug cards, a stream survey, and many ideas for projects.

NATIONAL WILDLIFE FEDERATION (1400 16th St. N.W., Washington, DC 20036; 202-797-6800) offers a backyard habitat information packet. This packet includes a booklet on how to attract wildlife, Craig Tuft's *The Backyard Naturalist,* and an application for certification in backyard habitat principles. To order call 800-432-6564, item #79919, $2.00 plus $2.95 for shipping and handling. Information on National Wildlife camps and conservation summits for the entire family is also available.

NATURE CONSERVANCY (1815 N. Lynn St., Arlington, VA 22209; 703-841-5300) offers a free information packet that includes information on the importance of maintaining species' diversity.

SIERRA CLUB (730 Polk St., San Francisco, CA 94109, 415-776-2211) will send The Source Book, a guide to all information and materials the Sierra Club has to offer.

TREES FOR LIFE (1103 Jefferson, Wichita, KS 67203; 316-263-7294) offers a tree-planting packet that includes seeds, instructions, a bumper sticker, and an activity booklet for $2 plus $2 for postage and handling. Buttons are available for $1 ("Let There Be Trees," "Kids Care," and "Trees for Life"). Free coloring books are also available.

U.S. DEPARTMENT OF AGRICULTURE (Soil Conservation Service, P.O. Box 2890, Washington, DC 20013; 202-720-5157) offers many free materials for children on soil conservation.

U.S. DEPARTMENT OF AGRICULTURE (U.S. Forest Service, P.O. Box 96090, Washington, DC 20250; 202-205-0957) has free posters available: "Why Leaves Change Color" and "How a Tree Grows."

U.S. DEPARTMENT OF ENERGY (Conservation and Renewable Energy Inquiry Referral Service, P.O. Box 8900, Silver Spring, MD 20907; 800-523-2929) has free information available for children and young adults on recycling, solar energy, renewable energy, and energy conservation.

WORLD WILDLIFE FUND (1250 24th St. N.W., Washington, DC 20037; 202-293-4800) will send fact sheets about endangered species and rain forests free of charge.

Bibliography

Commoner, Barry. *Making Peace with the Planet.* New York: Pantheon Books, 1990.

The Earth Works Group. *50 Simple Things You Can Do to Save the Earth.* Berkeley: Earthworks Press, 1989.

Elkington, John; Julia Hailes; and Joel Makower. *The Green Consumer.* New York: Penguin Books, 1990.

Elkington, John, and others. *Going Green: A Kid's Handbook to Saving the Planet.* New York: Puffin Books, 1990.

Goldstein, Jerome. *Recycling: How to Reuse Wastes in Home, Industry, and Society.* New York: Schocken Books, 1979.

Javna, John. *50 Simple Things Kids Can Do to Save the Earth.* Kansas City and New York: Andrews and McMeel, 1990.

Kelly, Katie. *Garbage.* New York: Saturday Review Press, 1973.

Luoma, Jon R. "Trash Can Realities," *Audubon,* XCII (March 1990): 86-97.

Michigan Department of Natural Resources. *Waste Information Series for Education.* Lansing, 1990.

Newsday, Inc. *Rush to Burn.* Washington, DC: Island Press, 1989.

O'Conner, Karen. *Garbage.* San Diego: Lucent Books, 1989.

Steger, Will, and Jon Bowermaster. *Saving the Earth: A Citizen's Guide to Environmental Action.* New York: Alfred A. Knopf, 1990.

White, Peter T. "The Fascinating World of Trash," *National Geographic,* CLXIII (April 1983): 424-56.

Wild, Russell (ed.). *The Earth Care Annual 1990.* Emmaus, PA: Rodale Press.

Wild, Russell (ed.). *The Earth Care Annual 1991.* Emmaus, PA: Rodale Press.

Answer to puzzle on page 15

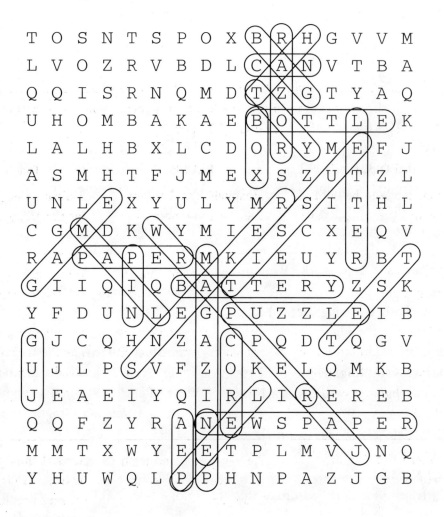

T O S N T S P O X B R H G V V M
L V O Z R V B D L C A N V T B A
Q Q I S R N Q M D T Z G T Y A Q
U H O M B A K A E B O T T L E K
L A L H B X L C D O R Y M E F J
A S M H T F J M E X S Z U T Z L
U N L E X Y U L Y M R S I T H L
C G M D K W Y M I E S C X E Q V
R A P A P E R M K I E U Y R B T
G I I Q I Q B A T T E R Y Z S K
Y F D U N L E G P U Z Z L E I B
G J C Q H N Z A C P Q D T Q G V
U J L P S V F Z O K E L Q M K B
J E A E I Y Q I R L I R E R E B
Q Q F Z Y R A N E W S P A P E R
M M T X W Y E E T P L M V J N Q
Y H U W Q L P P H N P A Z J G B

Answer to puzzle on page 52

It's Earthcare Jeopardy

Each phrase answers the question, "What is (are) _____ ?"
All the answers are in this book. See how many you know without looking
them up. A perfect score is 3,000 points.

POINTS	REDUCE	REUSE	RECYCLE
100	Things made to be used once and then thrown away. *disposables*	Hospitals like these for their waiting rooms. *magazines*	Broken glass, gathered for remelting. *cullet*
200	What we can say to over-packaged goods. *no*	Cutoffs, napkins, dust rags, etc. *recycled clothes*	Very expensive to mine, yet easy to recycle. *aluminum*
300	The number of homes that our discarded paper and wood could heat for 20 years. *50 million*	Salvation Army, Goodwill Industries, etc. *places we can bring (good) clothes we don't wear*	The number of trees saved when one ton of paper is recycled. *17*
400	An alternative to a disposable battery. *rechargeable battery*	An event at which trash is reduced, and wealth is spread. *a garage sale*	Aerosol cans, juice boxes, and plastic squeeze bottles. *things that can't be recycled*

More Ideas?

Write your ideas here and share them with friends.